aBOUT THE aUTHOR:

Reed Duncan is an author as well as a former
reading instructor, teacher, and school administrator.
He lives in Vermont. The Rollo stories are based on
Reed and his real-life, rambunctious bulldog,
who makes all kinds of barking, yawning, and
slurping noises.

For Lily, a very good girl—KF

PENGUIN WORKSHOP
An Imprint of Penguin Random House LLC, New York

Text copyright © 2020 by Reed Duncan. Illustrations copyright © 2020
by Penguin Random House LLC. All rights reserved. First published in hardcover in 2020
by Penguin Workshop. This paperback edition published in 2021 by Penguin Workshop,
an imprint of Penguin Random House LLC, New York. PENGUIN and PENGUIN WORKSHOP
are trademarks of Penguin Books Ltd, and the W colophon is
a registered trademark of Penguin Random House LLC.
Manufactured in China.

Visit us online at www.penguinrandomhouse.com.

Library of Congress Control Number: 2020948491

ISBN 9781524792534   10 9 8 7 6 5 4 3 2 1

LOOK AT ROLLO!

by REED DUNCAN
illustrated by KEITH FRAWLEY

PENGUIN WORKSHOP

Look at Rollo! He is waking up.

He is round.
He is brown.
He is very messy.

This is how Rollo says "Good morning."

BRAWK!

That's a funny way to say
"Good morning!"

Rollo likes to play at the park.

He always knows just how to catch the ball.

Or does he . . . ?

Look at Rollo go. Look at all the slobber!

Run, Rollo!

That's too slow.

Can he find the ball?

But now the ball is all wet!

Rollo is tired from playing.
He needs a nap.

Look at him napping.
He is quiet when he naps.
Snnn . . .

So very quiet.

SNNN . . .

Or is he . . . ?

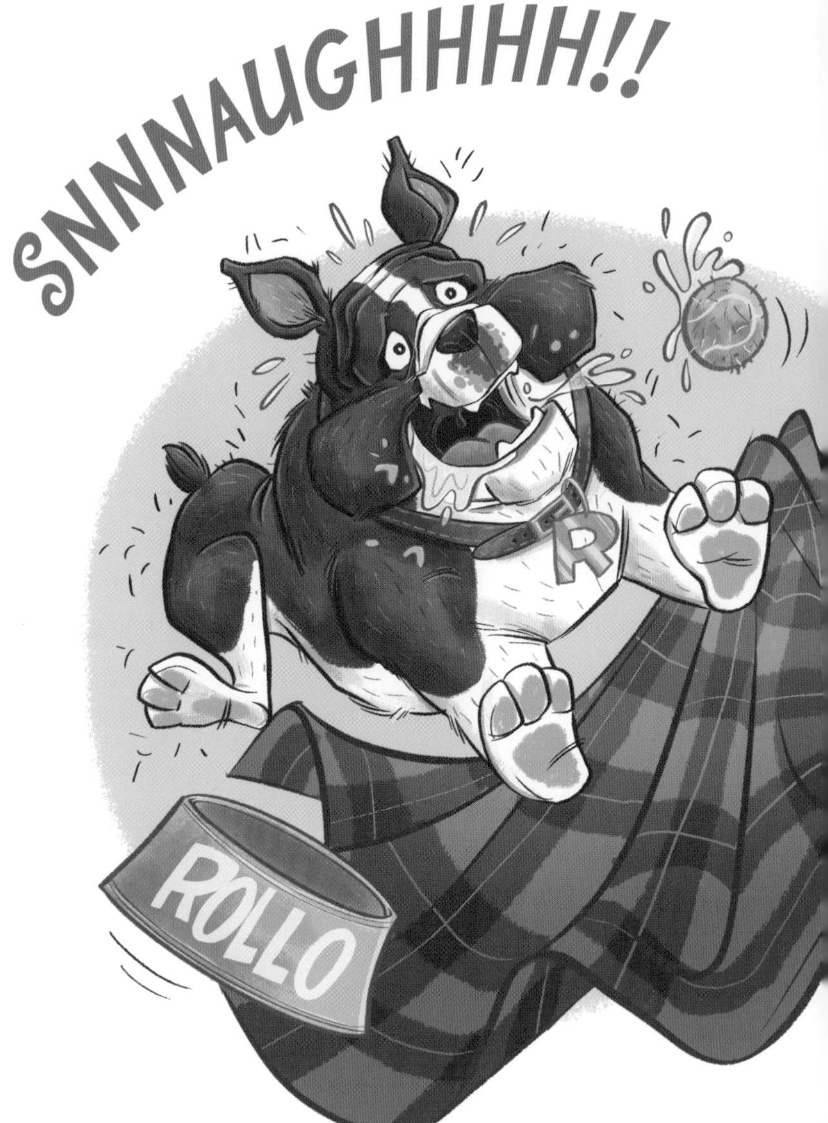
SNNNAUGHHHH!!
ROLLO

Look! Rollo woke himself up.

Rollo is hungry after his nap.

Look at Rollo eating!

He is a bit of a messy eater.

And a messy drinker.

But look!
Now he is all clean.

After such a busy day,
it's time for Rollo to go back home.

YAAWWWWWWNN.
Look how tired Rollo is.

It's time to go to bed.

This is how Rollo kisses "Good night."
SLUUURRRRRP!

He's a messy kisser, too!

Look! Rollo is sleeping in my lap.
Or is he . . . ?

Good night, Rollo!